Hansel
and Gretel

Other brilliant stories to collect:

Aesop's Fables
Malorie Blackman

The Goose Girl
Gillian Cross

The Snow Queen
Berlie Doherty

The Twelve Dancing
Princesses
Anne Fine

Grey Wolf, Prince Jack
and the Firebird
Alan Garner

The Three Heads in
the Well
Susan Gates

The Six Swan Brothers
Adèle Geras

The Seal Hunter
Tony Mitton

Cockadoodle-doo,
Mr Sultana!
Michael Morpurgo

Mossycoat
Philip Pullman

Rapunzel
Jacqueline Wilson

Rumpelstiltskin
Kit Wright

Hansel and Gretel

Retold by
Henrietta Branford

Illustrated by
Lesley Harker

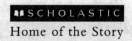
Home of the Story

Scholastic Children's Books,
Commonwealth House, 1–19 New Oxford Street,
London WC1A 1NU, UK
a division of Scholastic Ltd
London ~ New York ~ Toronto ~ Sydney ~ Auckland
Mexico City ~ New Delhi ~ Hong Kong

First published by Scholastic Ltd, 1998

Text copyright © Henrietta Branford, 1998
Illustrations copyright © Lesley Harker, 1998

ISBN 0 590 54383 0

Printed by The Bath Press, Bath

6 8 10 9 7 5

The right of Henrietta Branford and Lesley Harker to be identified as
the author and illustrator respectively of this work has been asserted
by them in accordance with the Copyright, Designs and
Patents Act, 1988.

There was once a poor woodcutter who lived with his two young children and their stepmother on the edge of a great forest. I don't know his name, nor that of his wife, but the children's names were Hansel and Gretel.

At first the forest was all quiet

mossy green below, with the soft rustle-bustle of the leaves above. But there came a summer when the sun shone hot and yellow day after day. Nice, you might think. And so it was, at first. But by and by the streams turned to trickles and the ponds became puddles and the earth grew hard and cracked. Fields turned yellow and then brown. Animals died for want of a mouthful of grass. People, too, grew hungry and afraid.

The woodcutter could neither work nor sleep for worrying about his children. "What can we do?" he asked

his wife. "We have no food, we have nothing for the children."

"Go fishing," said his wife. So he did. He caught the last little fish in the river. After that fish was gone, the family sat looking at the fish bones. The children would have liked to suck the bones, but, "Go to bed, children," snapped their stepmother. "There's nothing more for you to eat." She had half a loaf of mouldy bread hidden, but she meant to keep that for herself.

Hansel and Gretel went to bed hungry. When they had gone, their stepmother took the bones from the

pot and sniffed them. She looked at her husband. "Two people could live for longer than four on the juice of these bones," she said.

"Maybe so," said her husband, "but there are four of us."

"Then the children must go," said she.

"Never!" cried her husband. "How can you think of such a thing?"

"Don't be so soft!" snapped his wife. "We'll take them out into the forest, you can build them a fire and I will leave them half a crust I've got hidden. It's the only way."

"No!" cried the woodcutter. "Never! Nohow! That I will not do!"

"Do it, or we'll all be dead in a week," hissed his wife. "Do it if you love me." And that's how she went on.

At last her husband agreed to do what she wanted. "Good," smiled his wife. "I knew you'd see sense in the end. Come to bed now and be cosy. Once it is done, you won't have to worry about them any more."

Lying upstairs in their beds, Hansel and Gretel had heard every word. Hansel hopped out of bed and snuggled in beside his sister. "Don't be afraid," he said. "I shall look after you. I know how to keep us both safe." He crept downstairs, pulled on his jacket and peeped out at the moonlit garden. Everything in it was dead. Only the smooth white stones that lined the path shone milky white

like pearls. Hansel picked up a pocketful and crept back to bed.

Early next morning the children's stepmother shook them awake. "Get up!" she shouted. "Get washed! Get dressed! We're off to cut wood in the forest."

Their father picked up his axe and his saw. He wiped his eyes on his sleeve. Then he and his wife took Hansel and Gretel deep into the quiet green forest. They took them around and about, and around and about, until the children were quite lost. Every now and then Hansel hung

back, looking over his shoulder.

"Why do you keep stopping, Hansel, and looking back towards the house?" asked his stepmother.

"I'm looking back to see my white cat," Hansel answered. "He's up on the roof of our house, saying goodbye to me."

"Stupid boy," snapped his stepmother, tugging his arm. "That's not your white cat, it's just the morning sun shining on the chimney."

Hansel didn't answer. He hadn't been looking at his white cat anyway. He had been laying a trail with his smooth white stones to show him the way home.

By and by, when the children could walk no further, their father built them a fire of sticks and pine cones. "Rest here and warm yourselves," he said. "We're going to cut wood. Stay by the fire, don't wander. The forest is a wicked place."

"Come on," said his wife. "Hurry. It will soon be dark." She gave the children a corner of crust. "There'll be no more where that came from,"

she told them. "So don't eat it all at once." Husband and wife hurried away under the trees.

The sun sank low and the forest grew dark, with here a rustle, there a bustle, here a sniff, there a snuff, and everywhere a patter. Hansel and Gretel were very much afraid, but they lay down together by the fire and at last they slept.

When they woke up, the fire was out and the forest all around them was as dark as the inside of a cupboard. "They've gone and left us all alone," whispered Gretel.

"I know," said Hansel. "But I shall bring us both safe home. You'll see."

When the moon sailed up into the sky, her beams lit up the round white stones like pearls on a string. Away ran Hansel and Gretel, down the pearly path to home, and got there just in time to find their stepmother finishing the fish-bone soup.

"Lazy, disobedient children!" she

gasped. "Why did you sleep so long by the fire?" Their father said nothing, but took them in his arms and held them close.

That night the children lay in their beds again, listening to their stepmother. "This time there's nothing left at all," she said. "Not so much as a fish bone. It's them or us. You know I'm right."

"I'd rather we shared what we have, even if it's nothing, than take them back into the forest," said her husband.

"That's stupid!" snapped his wife. "How can you share nothing? Besides, you agreed to it the first time, so you must agree to it the second time."

Upstairs in their beds, Hansel and Gretel heard it all. "Don't worry, Gretel," whispered Hansel. "I'll keep us safe, just as I did before." He crept from his bed and tiptoed downstairs. He put up his hand to lift the latch

but the door would not open. His stepmother had locked it and hidden the key. Hansel crept back to bed.

Early next morning their stepmother shook the children up and out of bed. There was nothing but the end of a mouldy crust for breakfast.

"Don't eat it now, you'll want it later," said their stepmother. And they set off once more, walking deep

into the forest.

Again Hansel dawdled, looking back towards his home. "What's the good of looking back, Hansel?" his stepmother asked. "You know we must go on."

"I'm looking at my pigeon," said Hansel. "He's up on our roof saying goodbye to me."

"Daft boy!" scolded his stepmother. "That's not your pigeon, it's the morning sun shining on the chimney-pot."

Hansel didn't answer. He hadn't been looking at his pigeon anyway.

He had been laying a trail of crumbs
to show him the way home.

By and by they stopped, and their
father built a fire. He told the children to wait while he went off to cut
wood. "We'll be gone a good while,"
he said. "Remember that there are
wild animals in the forest. Stay close
to the fire."

This time Hansel and Gretel were

even more afraid, but at last they slept, lapped in the warmth of the burning embers. When they woke up, night shadows filled the forest. Wood shifted on the dying fire and sparks whirled up into the sky. An old hedgehog came up with a rustle and a snuffle, stopped to look at the two children, sitting so small and lonely under the stars, and trotted on. Soon it was quite dark. The children looked at one another.

"They've gone," said Gretel. "Haven't they?"

"I'm hungry," said Hansel.

"I saved my corner of crust. I'll give you half if you like."

"I used mine up to make us a trail of crumbs, Gretel. Wait till the moon comes out and then you'll see."

But when the moon came out there was no trail of crumbs. Ants had carried them off. Birds had pecked them up. Lumbering black beetles had clicked their pincers and gobbled them down. They were gone.

Away went Hansel and Gretel, hand in hand, searching all the dark night for a way out of the forest. They walked all night and all the next day, but they could not find a path to lead them home.

By the end of the third day they were too tired to walk any further. They lay down together and shut their eyes. High above the branches, the moon looked down on them and smiled. But the moon was not the only one out and about that night. A witch flew by on her broomstick, nosing here, sniffing there, searching for

lost lonely travellers. She found the sleeping children and whispered a spell into their ears:

"Sleep on, pretty children, sleep,
In the magic forest deep,
You are hungry, I am too;
There's no one to take care of you.
Sleep on, pretty children, sleep,
In the magic forest deep.
When you wake up you will find
Sweets and treats of every kind,
Search for them and you will see;
Pretty children, come to me."

When Hansel and Gretel woke up, they felt strange; very strange. "There's something tugging at me," said Gretel.

"I feel it too," whispered Hansel. "It's tugging at my hungriness."

"Let's look for it," said Gretel.

The children set off through the forest, drawn on close and tight by the witch's spell. By and by they came to

a dear little house all made of chocolate and toffee and biscuits and sweets, with a roof of cake and a lawn of sugar frosting. There was a lollipop fence and a toffee-apple tree and a sweet soda fountain with a flock of ice-cream ducks. The children could hardly believe their luck.

The witch, too, was delighted. Up in the attic, where Hansel and Gretel could not see her, she licked her lips. A black cat twined around her legs, mewing softly.

Hansel and Gretel ran towards the house. They couldn't wait to gulp

down cake and sugar, to stuff their mouths with chocolate and toffee, to scoop up soda and lick up ice-cream ducks. Gretel broke off the flap of the letter-box and sat down to enjoy it.

Just as she sat down, a little creaking voice called out:

> *"Nibble, nibble little mouse,*
> *Who is gnawing at my house?"*

Gretel put down her letter-box flap and answered bravely:

"It is not I, it is not I
It is the wind, child of the sky."

And she took another bite.

The witch came down from the attic and poked her nose out of the door. When her black cat saw the children, he unsheathed his cruel claws and his cold green eyes shone like emeralds.

"Come in, my dears," smiled the witch. "Sit by my fire while I put food on the table and make up warm, soft beds. Come in, why not?"

Should they go in? No. Never!

But, "Thank you," said Gretel. And, "Yes please," said Hansel. And in they went. The moment they stepped inside that house, chocolate and toffee disappeared, and all the biscuits and the sweets and the lollipop fence and the toffee-apple tree, the sweet soda fountain and the ice-cream ducks. That house was made of nothing but sticks and mud. There was no food on the table and there were no warm beds. There was just a heap of rags beside an iron cage. Hansel and Gretel looked at the old woman. She didn't look kind any more. Too late,

Hansel and Gretel understood. But before they could turn and run, the witch caught Hansel by the neck and bundled him into the cage and banged the door shut and locked it with an iron key.

"Get up!" she hissed at Gretel. "Get up and get to work! I want a good cooked breakfast and I want it NOW! No, I want two – one for me and one for your brother. I shall soon fatten him up – and when he's fat enough I'll eat him!"

That's how it was. Hansel stayed locked in the cage and every day Gretel cooked porridge to fatten him up — but not one mouthful of it did she taste herself. No. The old woman gave her nothing but mouldy green bread. "Your turn comes later," she would say. "After I've eaten your brother." The black cat watched from his place by the fire, smiling a black cat smile.

Every morning the witch would rattle the bars of Hansel's cage. "Stick your finger through the bars," she'd say. "Let me squeeze it. Are you getting fat?"

Every morning Hansel pushed out an old bone that he'd found on the floor of his cage. The witch, whose eyesight was very poor, would pinch the bone between her fingers, and frown, and shake her head. "Gretel!"

she'd shout. "You're a rotten cook!
Your brother is no more than skin and
bone, there's not a decent mouthful
on him!"

Gretel would cook more porridge.
What else could she do? She was in the
witch's power. And Hansel would eat
it, though he hated porridge. He grew
fat and slow, shut up in his cage.

Round about midnight every
night, the witch would wake up her
cat and call up her broomstick and go
out and away, locking the door behind
her. While she was gone, Gretel would
search for the iron key that might

unlock her brother. She even searched the witch's bedroom. There was a great high bed made of bones and a pumpkin head beside it with a candle for a light. It seemed to be laughing at Gretel. Old clothes, odd shoes, and pairs of spectacles spilled out from under the bed. Gretel would search as best she could but the key didn't want to be found. At last she would sit down next to Hansel's cage. They would hold hands through the bars and do their best to comfort one another. "I'll find it in the end, Hansel, I know I will," Gretel would

promise. "And when I do, we'll run away together."

Time passed in the dark house, slow as sorrow, until one dark and stormy night, the witch called up her cat as usual, mounted her broomstick and away they went, skimming over the treetops, weaving through the thickets, poking into hollow places, sniffing and spying for lost lonely travellers.

Back in the house, the fire went out. The room grew pitchy dark. Gretel crept out from under her rags. She lit a candle and she searched the whole house but still she found no key. By and by she pressed herself to Hansel's cage. The children leaned close and held each other's hands tight, tight against the dark.

"It's now or never, Gretel," whispered Hansel. "You must run away tonight. The witch is hungry for me, I can tell. She won't wait much longer. Go now, tonight. Go quickly before she comes back!"

"Where would I run to, without you, Hansel?"

"Anywhere. There can't be a worse place than this."

"What about you, Hansel?"

"I must stay here and face what's coming to me."

"Not on your own, though. Never on your own. We'll face what comes together."

Then came a thumping and bumping from up on the roof. "Too late, Gretel," whispered Hansel. "Quick – into bed." Gretel crept under her pile of rags and shut her eyes just as the

witch slid down the chimney and into the room, shaking the soot from her hair. She had caught nothing and nobody all night and she was tired and hungry.

She went to Hansel's cage and rattled the bars. Hansel pushed the old bone out for her to feel: it was just as thin as ever. "Wake up Gretel!" shouted the witch. "Wake up, you ugly waste of space! Your brother hasn't gained so much as a slick or a sliver of fat! Get up and light the fire! Heat up the oven! Today we'll cook him, fat or thin!"

Gretel could hardly see to light
the fire, she cried so hard. But she lit
it just the same. What else could she
do? And Hansel watched her, know-
ing what the fire was for. By and by
the logs glowed red and the old brick
oven grew hot and the witch, thinking
of the feast to come, grew hungry.

"*One* may not be enough," she said
to her black cat. "*Two* would certainly
be better." The black cat licked his
lips. "Gretel," said the witch, "lean
into the oven and tell me if it's hot
enough."

"Yes, Auntie," said Gretel. And

she peeped in. "I think it's hot enough," she said, "but there's something sitting in there, right at the back of the oven. What can it be?"

"Out of my way, stupid, and let me look," shouted the witch.

"Certainly, Auntie, right away," said Gretel. "*You* lean in and look."

The moment the witch leaned in, Gretel gave her an almighty shove. In went the witch, slam bang into her very own oven. Gretel shut the oven door tight and stood beside it, shaking.

Well, that was the end of the witch. It was the end of the black cat

too: he turned to soot and cinders and floated up the chimney. And there, right where he'd been sitting, lay the key to the cage. Gretel picked it up and slid it into the lock. She turned it carefully. The door swung open with a groan and out jumped Hansel, into Gretel's arms. They hugged and they hugged and they hugged one another. Then they sat down to think.

"All witches have hidden treasure," Hansel said, when he had thought enough. "Let's look for hers." The children tipped up boxes, swept crockery crashing off shelves, tore

down curtains, ripped up clothes, threw spell books to burn on the fire, and sent potions and lotions swirling away in a sticky black pall of smoke that blotted out the sky – but only for a moment.

When the whole house was in a fine mess and muddle, Hansel's eye fell on the witch's coal box. He kicked it over with the toe of his boot and out rolled the coal, all over the carpet. And after the coal, something else. Something shiny – a big old silver box. Gretel took a knife and prised it open.

That box was *stuffed* with gold and silver coins, with rings and earrings and necklaces and jewels of all kinds, taken from the ears and the fingers and the pockets of all the people the witch had eaten, down all the many hundred years she'd lived in that dark house. There were diamonds and rubies, emeralds, sapphires, blood red coral and milky white pearls. There was even a little jewelled watch, still ticking softly.

The children filled their pockets with treasures of every kind. Then away they ran, hand in hand under

the rustling leaves. When they stopped to look back, the witch's house was gone. All that remained was a little pile of ashes. Foxgloves were already growing through them, green against the grey.

After a mile or two, Hansel and Gretel came to a rushing river. "I'm sure our home is on the other side," said Hansel. "But how can we cross over?"

"Someone will help us," said
Gretel.

No sooner had she spoken than
two white swans came swimming up-
river with the water lap-lapping and
the soft foam curling round their
breast feathers.

"Father Swan, Mother Swan, we
need to cross the river. Will you help
us?" Gretel asked.

The swans looked at Gretel out of
their wise black eyes. They nodded
their sleek heads and spoke to one
another in swan language, which is
silent. Then they swam to the bank

and waited while the children climbed on to their backs.

When they reached the far bank, Hansel and Gretel thanked the swans politely and set off to search for home.

By and by the forest began to look familiar. Hansel and Gretel began to run. Before long they could see their father's house away in the distance. They pelted down the path and through the garden, right to their own front doorstep. The door stood open. There at the table sat their father, carving a piece of wood into the likeness of his two lost children.

When he looked up and saw Hansel and Gretel standing in the doorway, he smiled the first smile he'd smiled since the dreadful day he left them alone in the forest. It was the biggest, longest smile he'd ever smiled.

Hansel and Gretel jumped into his arms. When they had finished hugging, they emptied their pockets out on to the kitchen table. There lay the treasure, shining in the sunlight. It wasn't magic and it didn't disappear. But what about their cruel stepmother? Well, she wasn't there any more.

At the very same moment when the witch died in the forest, so did the wicked stepmother.

And what happened next? Well, Hansel and Gretel and their father lived happily ever after – and they were never hungry again. And that's all that I can tell you.